Scully tri[illegible]
"I can see them – [illegible]

She led the way to the tarp. Dots of green [illegible] glowed through the dirty plastic. Hundreds of dots.

"They're coming through the walls," Scully said. "Down near the floor. Where the light doesn't reach. I want to get a better look at them."

With the others looking over her shoulder, Scully pressed down both hands against the tarp. She started smoothing away the wrinkles.

"Aaaaah!" she screamed.

The glowing green dots were on her arm, crawling up it.

"They're on me!" she shrieked. "Get them off!"

Other X-Files books

#1 X Marks the Spot
#2 Darkness Falls
#3 Tiger, Tiger
#4 Squeeze
#5 Humbug

Voyager

THE X FILES™

DARKNESS FALLS

A novel by Les Martin

Based on the television series *The X-Files* created by Chris Carter

Based on the teleplay written by Chris Carter

HarperCollins*Publishers*

Voyager
An Imprint of HarperCollins*Publishers*
77–85 Fulham Palace Road,
Hammersmith, London W6 8JB

This paperback edition 1997
First paperback edition 1996
1 2 3 4 5 6 7 8 9

First published in the USA by HarperTrophy
A division of HarperCollins*Publishers* 1995

Cover photo by Michael Grecco

ISBN 0 583 33482 2

Set in Century

Printed in Great Britain by
Caledonian International Book Manufacturing Ltd, Glasgow

Chapter ONE

Dense morning fog filled the forest.

It curled like gray smoke around the thick trunks of evergreens hundreds of feet tall.

It swirled around the bushes and brambles of the undergrowth.

It blanketed the carpet of pine needles on the forest floor.

The shrouded forest was as still as death. The only sound was the croaking of a lone tree frog.

It could have been a scene hundreds and hundreds of years ago. When the trees were slender saplings. When only Native Americans lived here on the Pacific coast.

That was before pale-skinned strangers arrived. And made this territory one of the United States. And named it after their first president. The state of Washington.

Now, in the 1990s, new strangers had come to the forest. Men who made their livings from it. Loggers. They stood in a clearing that they had made themselves. Around them were stumps of trees they had felled.

There were thirty of them. All of them were as

hard and tough as the iron and steel in their axes and power saws. All of them were used to dealing with every challenge and danger of the wilderness.

And all of them now were shaking in their boots.

Jack Dyer was the man they looked to as leader. His voice boomed through the mist. "This thing could kill us all!"

A big, burly logger named Bob Perkins answered, "I told you we should have cleared out two days ago! But no! You wouldn't listen! Dyer, remember what you called me? Chicken. So tell me, who's squawking now?"

Dyer strode over to Perkins. They stood glaring face-to-face. Their callused hands were clenched in white-knuckled fists.

Then Dyer dropped his hands. "No sense in slugging each other," he said. "We got bigger fish to fry. If I could only get my hands on it, I'd—" His hands opened and closed on empty air.

Perkins would not let go of his anger before taking another shot. "Still Mr. Macho Man, huh? Just like two days ago."

"Nobody knew what it was two days ago, Perkins," Dyer snapped. Then he shook his head. "Nobody knows now."

"Somebody's got to go for help," Perkins said.

His idea stirred bitter muttering and sour laughter from the other loggers.

Dyer spoke for them. "And what about the rest of us?" he demanded. "What are we supposed to do? Wait here until help arrives?"

"We have to take a chance," Perkins insisted. "One of us has to hike out."

"That person might not make it in time. He might not get to the road before nightfall. Then what?" Dyer asked.

Perkins did not answer. He did not have to. They all knew what to expect if you were still in the forest when darkness fell.

Dyer turned to the others. "I say we make a run for it. Split up and take our chances."

Perkins opened his mouth to argue.

Before he could, one man shouted, "It's our last chance!"

"No more nights here!" shouted another.

"Each man for himself! Sink or swim!" a third joined in.

Perkins made a last try. "It's suicide! You know that as well as me, Dyer!"

"Fine," Dyer said. "You stay here tonight and let us know how things come out."

Dyer was already unbuckling the heavy belt he used for climbing trees.

Around him the others did the same.

Nobody wanted anything to slow him down. They were all in a race. A race through the forest against the sun moving above the tall trees. A race against nightfall.

Late that afternoon, Dyer was still running. Or trying to. He had a stitch in his side. It felt like a spike driving into him. His legs felt like stone. His mouth tasted like pennies. Every breath hurt. But the sight of the daylight dimming through the branches above was enough to keep him lurching forward.

Dyer wondered how the others were doing. He didn't figure they were much better off than he. He wished now that they had stayed together. Maybe you traveled faster when you traveled alone. But you also got more scared. He had never felt so alone and scared in his life.

"Owww," he screamed. His cry echoed through the silent forest.

He had tripped over a fallen branch. His body fell forward, but his foot stayed wedged under the branch. He could almost hear his ankle crack.

He tried to keep tears of pain from his eyes. He got his foot free of the branch. He eased himself into a sitting position. He unlaced his boot. He gingerly eased it off.

"Is it bad?" asked a voice.

Perkins was looking down at him. His chest was heaving.

"I think it's broken," Dyer said.

"Come on," Perkins told him. "You gotta get up."

Dyer put his hand on his ankle. He winced. "I don't think I can make it," he said.

"I told you, come on," Perkins said.

He put his arms under Dyer's shoulders. With a grunting heave, he lifted Dyer to his feet.

"Put your arm around my shoulder," Perkins said. "We'll make it out of here together."

"Thanks," Dyer said. "But why are you doing this? You know you hate my guts."

"Forget about that," Perkins said. "Maybe we have our differences. But at least we're humans. And right now humans have to stick together."

"Yeah," said Dyer. "I remember what old Ben Franklin said. I learned it in history when I was a kid. 'We gotta hang together—or else we'll hang separately.' Except it won't be hanging for us. It won't be so nice."

"Come on. Enough jawing," said Perkins. "It's getting dark already."

They started moving again. But they couldn't go fast. Three legs weren't enough for two men. They staggered like a mechanical toy with a part missing.

"How many more miles, you think?" Dyer panted.

"No idea," Perkins gasped back. "Wish there were some landmarks here."

"You hear that?" Dyer said. He stopped moving.

He listened to a distant humming.

"Insects, just insects," Perkins said. "They come out in the dark."

"And it is dark now, isn't it," said Dyer. He stayed frozen. "We can't make it."

The humming got closer, louder.

"Guess old Ben was wrong," Dyer said. "Hang together—and die together."

"No!" said Perkins. "We ain't giving up!"

He yanked Dyer forward, half dragging him along.

But the humming was all around them now. And the forest around them was growing bright.

Perkins looked up. Through the treetops the darkness was gone, replaced by a dazzling cloud of whirling green light. Perkins' shoulders slumped. He let Dyer go.

Dyer fell to his knees. Perkins stood over him, trying to shield him, as the blinding light descended.

The humming was deafening.

It drowned out the last human sounds in the forest.

Perkins' screams of pain.

Chapter TWO

"It's show and tell time, Scully," F.B.I. Agent Fox Mulder said. "Come into my office."

"Said the spider to the fly," replied F.B.I. Agent Dana Scully. She finished the last bite of her doughnut. She took the last sip of her coffee. Then she left the F.B.I. Headquarters basement cafeteria with Mulder. They headed down the long corridor toward his office.

Scully braced herself for what was coming. She recognized the gleam in Mulder's eyes. Mulder had spotted a case that interested him. A case that belonged in the X-files. A case that nobody in the Bureau wanted to touch. Nobody except Mulder..

The X-files contained cases that the F.B.I. brass called strange, weird, bizarre—in short, nutty. They would have liked to lock the X-files up and throw away the key. Mulder, however, kept opening them up.

For the F.B.I. brass, that was bad enough. Even worse, Mulder had too brilliant a record to be dismissed as a loose cannon. His bosses had to find another way to protect their peace of mind. They did. They made Scully his partner.

Scully had what it took to do the job. She was

not only a doctor, she was a scientist as well. She had the knowledge and skills to check out Mulder's theories about unknown aliens spreading havoc on earth. And she had plenty of down-to-earth common sense. Enough of it to keep Mulder from going completely out of orbit. As a last resort, Scully was there for damage control. Her bosses told her to blow the whistle the moment Mulder started acting as freaky as the cases he loved. Except by now Scully was no longer following that set of orders. By now, Scully had worked on Mulder's side long enough and hard enough to start seeing through Mulder's eyes.

Right now Scully could barely keep up with Mulder's eager stride. Out of the corner of her eye she saw heads turn as they hurried past. She knew tongues would start wagging as fellow agents wondered what they were up to. She wondered the same thing herself. With Mulder you never knew what the next case would bring. You could only wait and see.

"You've gotta see this," Mulder said as they entered his office. "It'll impress even you, Scully."

Scully had been in Mulder's office many times. But it still made her shudder.

Shelves lined the walls from floor to ceiling. Crammed on them were folders bulging with reports, stacks of yellowing newspapers and magazines, floppy disks with curling labels, and every kind of book from science textbooks to science-fiction paperbacks. Piled on the floor were more records and writings.

Scully liked neatness and order. This office was her notion of a nightmare. She had no idea how Mulder ever found anything he wanted. But he always seemed to.

Right now he had his slide projector loaded and his projection screen pulled down.

"Take a good look at this," he said, as a slide came onto the screen. It was a candid photo, a little blurred, showing a group of about thirty men. They had on well-worn outdoor gear. Most were bearded. Many held axes. In front of them was a huge fallen tree. Behind them stood a towering forest.

"Loggers, right?" Scully said.

"You've won the set of Tupperware," Mulder said. "Want to try for the microwave?"

"Come on, who are they?" Scully asked.

"A logging gang working in Washington," Mulder said.

"Washington?" Scully said. "I didn't know they had trees like that around here."

"Not Washington, D.C.," Mulder said. "The state of Washington. Now tell me, what else do you see?"

"They look tough," Scully said. "Men's men, I believe is the term."

"Very good," Mulder said. "And what else besides that. Anything strange? Out of the ordinary? Hard to explain?"

Scully took a hard look. She shook her head. "I give up," she said.

"You give up," Mulder said, nodding. "Funny. That's exactly what the Federal Forest Service has done."

"What do you mean?" Scully asked. "What happened to them?"

Mulder pressed a button. The photo vanished. "They vanished," he said.

He flashed on another photo. This one was of just two men. They wore bright flowered shirts, ragged blue jeans, scruffy high-tops. They had unkempt beards and long dirty-looking hair. One had his hair in a ponytail. The other had a bandanna tied around his forehead.

"They look like they're going to a 1960s costume party," Scully remarked. "All they need is bell-bottoms."

"Meet Douglas Spinney and Steven Teague," said Mulder. "They call themselves 'monkey-wrenchers.' And they're very good at what they do."

"What do they do?" Scully asked.

"Everything they can think of to foul up lumberjacks and lumber mills. One of their favorite things is driving spikes into trees to make saws break," Mulder said.

"Ecoterrorists," Scully said grimly. As an F.B.I. agent, she knew the type. People who claimed that they loved nature. That they were fighting for the environment. That it was okay to trash anyone and anything in the name of ecology. "Do-gooders who do bad things. They can be the worst."

"Teague and Spinney *are* the worst," said Mulder. "Two weeks ago, we got the latest word on them. The loggers I showed you in the first slide radioed from the middle of Olympic National Forest. Seems that Teague and Spinney went on a spree: spiking trees, wrecking equipment, the works. A week later, all radio communication was cut off."

"Anyone know why?" asked Scully.

"No," Mulder said. "The lumber company that hired the men asked the Federal Forest Service to check it out. Two officials went into the forest a week ago. Nobody has heard from them since."

"Looks like the monkeywrenchers aren't just playing games," Scully said. "They're playing for keeps."

"That's what the lumber company and the forest service say," Mulder said. "They've asked the Bureau to investigate. I had to pull strings to make sure we got the case."

"Pull strings? To get an ecoterrorism case?" Scully said, puzzled.

Then she saw Mulder grin, and braced herself.

"Dare I ask why you want this case so badly?" she asked.

"Take a look at this picture," he answered.

A new slide came up on the screen. It showed more loggers. Tough men, too. But their outdoor gear was old-fashioned.

"This was taken in 1934," Mulder said. "Long before ecoterrorism was even in the dictionary. This crew was working for a government agency, the WPA. They vanished in the same forest without a trace. Not one of them was ever found or heard from again."

"And you suspect what?" Scully asked. "Bigfoot, maybe?"

"Not likely," Mulder answered deadpan. "That's a lot of flannel to choke down. Even for Bigfoot."

Scully sighed. She should have known better than to joke about Bigfoot to Mulder. Bigfoot wasn't a joke to him.

"Come on, Scully," he responded cheerfully. "What could be nicer than a trip to the forest? I bet you were a Girl Scout when you were a kid."

Mulder was right as usual. Scully *had* been a Girl Scout. And she had earned every merit badge.

But those wouldn't be of much use to her now. Mulder's favorite territory—the uncharted regions of the X-files—wasn't covered by the Official Girl Scout Handbook. . . .

Chapter THREE

"I feel like an ad for L.L. Bean," Scully told Mulder. She was dressed in jeans, a flannel shirt, and hiking boots. All were brand-new.

"When in Rome," said Mulder. He was dressed the same way. But his clothes were broken in.

"Some Rome. More like nowhere," Scully said. She looked out the window of their rental car. Thick forest ran to both edges of the road. "I hope we're going in the right direction. They're not big on signs around here."

Scully was doing the driving, which she preferred. Mulder knew only two speeds: fast and faster.

Right now Scully would have liked to go faster herself. Crawling ahead of them on the narrow blacktop was a big flatbed, loaded high with huge logs.

"We're fine," Mulder said. "That truck is going to the same place we are. There's just one lumber mill around here. I hope the guy from the forest service is there. He said he'd be waiting for us."

"He's pals with the lumber company?" asked Scully.

"I don't know about being pals," Mulder said with a shug. "But they know each other. This is government forest. The forest service tells the lumber company where they can cut and how much."

They followed the flatbed as it turned off onto an even narrower road. Soon they saw the mill. And smelled it.

"Whew—what an odor," Scully said, closing her window. "I always thought sawdust smelled nice."

"They use a lot of chemicals to process the wood," Mulder said. "They say if you work here long enough, you stop noticing it."

"I guess you can get used to anything," Scully said. "Like in morgues. I've seen attendants playing cards on corpses. Probably folks around here have forgotten what clean air smells like."

"There aren't many folks around here," Mulder said. "That's why they put the mill out in the wilds. Otherwise they'd have protesters in front of the gates. And pressure to pass laws."

"I can understand that kind of environmental action," Scully said, as she found a spot in the mill parking lot. "Ecoprotest—not ecoterror."

She parked next to a four-wheel-drive truck. The truck was a wilderness special. It had mud tires, winches, bumper guards, a windshield screen, and the emblem of the Federal Forest Service on its front door.

A tall, lean man in outdoor gear stood by the truck. He had a map spread out on the hood.

"Looks like our boy," Scully said.

"Hi," Mulder said to the man by the truck. "Agent Mulder here. This is Agent Scully. We're with the F.B.I."

The man took his time looking Mulder and Scully up and down.

"Got identification?" he asked.

Mulder produced a photo ID from his wallet. Scully did the same.

The man glanced at the pictures, gave the two agents another slow look, and handed the IDs back. Then he stuck out his hand to shake Mulder's, then Scully's. He had a grip like iron.

"Larry Moore, Federal Forest Service," he said. "You can put your gear in the back of the truck."

"What's that on the windshield there?" Mulder asked. "A bullet hole?"

"Twenty-two calibre," Moore said shortly. He started folding up the map.

"Somebody shoot at you?" Mulder asked.

"That's what it would appear," Moore said. "Sure wasn't a hunter's stray shot. Not much to hunt around here with that kind of ammo. 'Cept Freddies."

"Freddies?" asked Scully.

"Employees of the Federal Forest Service,"

Moore said. "That's what the ecoterrorists call us."

"That who you think shot at you?" Mulder asked. "You have a problem with them?"

Moore fixed Mulder with a level gaze.

"Let's get this straight right now," he said. "I've got no beef with what those people claim they want. I want to save the forest, too. It's their methods I can't condone. There's never any reason to cause unlawful damage—not to mention taking human lives."

"Point taken," said Scully. "But you really think they'd go as far as killing?"

"There are over thirty men missing in the forest," Moore said. "All of them with survival experience. *Something* happened to them."

A station wagon pulled up on the other side of the truck. A big, muscular man got out.

He easily lifted two heavily loaded packs out of his car and tossed them into the back of the truck. Then he grabbed a couple of large containers from his front seat. Scully glimpsed what they were. Cases of shotgun shells.

"At last," Moore said. "Now we can get this show on the road."

"Sorry I'm late, Larry," said the man. "I was just down talking to Bob Perkins' wife." He turned to Mulder and Scully. "Perkins is one of our missing loggers," he explained.

Then he introduced himself. "Steve Humphreys. Head of security, Schiff-Immergut Lumber. You must be F.B.I."

"I'm Mulder," Mulder said. "She's Scully."

Humphreys gave them a nod. Then he handed the cases of shotgun shells to Moore. "Take good care of these," he said. "I have a hunch we could need them."

"Maybe," Moore said. He stowed the shells in the cab of the truck.

"Let's get rolling," said Humphreys. "Got about four hours driving ahead of us." He climbed into the truck, followed by Moore.

Scully turned to Mulder. "I have a feeling we're riding into a war," she told him. "A war that's already started."

Chapter FOUR

Scully knew that in a war, the first casualty was always the truth. Which made it all the harder to get the facts in this case. She couldn't take what Moore and Humphreys said as gospel. She'd have to decide for herself who were the bad guys and who the good. And so would Mulder.

Soon they left all signs of civilization behind. They turned off the highway onto a rutted dirt road. A loggers' road. It was just wide enough for a truck to squeeze through, and it led higher and higher up through the tree-covered mountains.

Scully and Mulder were squeezed in the front seat between Moore and Humphreys. The two F.B.I. agents used the long drive to start probing. They had worked together enough to be a good team.

"Why do the loggers work so far up in the wilderness?" began Scully.

"That's where the trees are," said Humphreys.

Scully looked out the window. All she saw were trees. All she had seen since they began were trees. "You're kidding, right?" she said.

"It's those environmentalists." Humphreys snorted. "They worry more about trees than about people. They've managed to keep us from touching a single branch around here. They make us go to the most remote spots to do our cutting. Even there, we have to replant saplings for every tree we take."

"So why do you think that the ecoterrorists are targeting you?" asked Mulder. "Seems they've gotten all they're after."

"Nothing is enough for them," said Humphreys. "Those tree huggers won't be happy until we can't touch a tree on the planet. Until we go out of business and our loggers go on welfare." He shook his head. "What gets me is they won't come out and fight like men. They're the kind who dodged the draft in the Vietnam war. They're cowardly and so are their tactics. I'd like to get my hands on them and—"

Bang! Bang! Two sharp explosions.

Instinctively Scully ducked her head, hands shielding her face. But there were no bullets, no flying glass. Instead, the truck bucked like a bronco. A moment later, it was lurching from side to side.

"What was that?" Scully asked Moore, as the forest service agent put on the brakes.

"Tires," Moore said. He did not look surprised. Just angry.

As soon as the truck stopped, he was out of the driver's cab. The others followed.

"I'll check the left side," Moore told Humphreys. "You take the right."

Scully and Mulder stood behind Moore as he kneeled by the left front wheel. The tire was flat as a pancake.

Moore pulled out a long sharp piece of metal. "Homemade tire spike," he said.

"Serious damage?" asked Scully.

"Right through the sidewall," Moore said. "Unfixable."

"You've got a spare, don't you?" Mulder asked.

Before Moore could answer, Humphreys came around to their side. "The right tire's history, too," he said.

He handed Mulder a bent piece of metal with four spikes sticking out of it. "Maybe you'd like to put this in the F.B.I. files," he said.

Mulder passed it to Scully. "Nasty-looking piece of work," she said.

"Monkeywrenchers call it a caltrop," Humphreys told her. "They litter these roads with them. Doesn't matter what comes over them. Blind terrorism pure and simple."

Scully handed the device back to him. Humphreys flung it into the trees.

"Imagine someone putting these down on the Washington, D.C., beltway," he said. "I'd like to see what lawmakers would do then. And how much sympathy these environmentalists would get."

Before Humphreys could say anything else,

Scully changed the subject. "How do we get to the loggers' camp now?" she asked.

"We do it the old-fashioned, low-tech way," Moore said. "We hike."

"Well, these boots were made for walking," Scully said. She looked ahead at the dirt road. It snaked upward through the forest, climbing out of sight. "I just hope the salesman was right."

Hours later, it was a toss-up whether Scully's feet were breaking in the boots—or vice versa. She wished she'd stuffed less in her backpack. A lot less. And she wondered how Mulder's step could still be springy. In the future, she decided, she'd up her daily jog to match his seven miles. Her usual three didn't cut it.

She breathed easier when she spotted a vehicle parked up the road.

"Signs of life at last," she said.

"Signs of something at least," said Moore.

"What kind of vehicle is it?" Mulder asked.

"A skiploader," Humphreys told him. "For lifting felled trees onto transport."

"But useless now," Moore said. He pointed to a giant flat tire. The blunt end of a spike stuck out of its sidewall. "Come on. The camp can't be far away."

The camp was ten minutes up the road. Two big logging trucks and a small crane came into sight first. Then a small wooden cabin. Beyond the cabin was a cluster of medium-size olive-green tents.

The open truck doors swung back and forth in the forest breeze, creaking eerily.

"Anybody here?" Moore shouted.

There was no answer.

"Brrr," Scully said to Mulder. "Looks like a ghost town."

Mulder headed for the cabin. Scully followed him inside.

"Somebody forgot to clean his plate," Mulder said. Moldy, half-eaten portions of food covered the crude wooden dining table.

"Maybe they got tired of franks and beans and went after bear," said Scully. She looked around the cabin. Chairs lay upended on the rough plank floor. The bunks in the other room were unmade. "Looks like they left in a hurry."

"And they forgot to pack," Mulder said, standing by the refrigerator. Its door was open. He reached in and pulled out a Ziploc bag. It was stuffed with tiny buds.

Scully took a quick look. "A controlled substance?" she asked.

Mulder sniffed one of the buds and nodded. "I guess loggers have to find a way to pass the long nights without TV."

He ran his finger over the top of the bag.

"Something interesting?" asked Scully.

"Some kind of grease," Mulder said.

He was still studying it when Humphreys came into the cabin.

"Find anything?" Humphreys asked.

"Party favors," Mulder said. "And you?"

"Vehicles have all been monkeywrenched," Humphreys said. "Power generator's busted."

"Somebody really did a number here," said Scully.

"And that somebody didn't want the news broadcast either," Humphreys said. He picked up what was left of a shortwave radio transmitter. It had been smashed to bits.

"Let's see what Moore's up to," Mulder suggested.

They found him at one of the trucks. He had lifted the hood and unscrewed the radiator cap.

"The radiator's full of rice," he said. "So are the others. Plus sugar and sand in the crankcases. Our pals didn't miss a trick."

"Wonder what else they pulled off," said Mulder.

"Not much more time to find out today," Humphreys said. He looked at his watch. "Sun's going down in an hour and a half."

"I'm taking another look around here before it gets dark," Moore said.

"You do that," Humphreys said. "I'll see if I can get the generator working."

As the two moved off, Scully peered into the radiator. Moore was right. Plump grains of rice filled the radiator. She fished out a few grains.

"Well, you were right about one thing," she told Mulder.

"What's that?" Mulder asked.

"It definitely wasn't Bigfoot."

Chapter FIVE

Mulder looked around at the camp. "Of course, we're not even sure *what* was done," he said. "Much less who did it."

"Yeah. It's like being in a cemetery with no corpses," said Scully. Then she said, "Here comes Moore. Maybe he's found something."

"Nothing here," the forest service agent reported. "Nothing that works. Or breathes. Those monkey-wrenchers made a clean sweep."

"We still don't have proof of that," Mulder said.

"Hard evidence is what we need," Scully agreed.

"We still have an hour of daylight," Moore said. "Enough time to check out the forest around here. Might turn up something."

"Good idea," said Scully. "The sooner we clean this case up and get out of here, the better. I have to admit, this place gives me the creeps."

"The creeps?" said Mulder with a smile. "Just because a bunch of big, strong men cleared out so fast they didn't finish their food? And then vanished into thin air? Don't be silly. I'm sure there's a nice scientific explanation. Oh, sorry, Scully. You're the one who's supposed to be telling me that, right?"

Scully winced. Mulder loved to remind her of what she had once told him. Everything had a scientific explanation. That was when she had first met him, before their first case together. That seemed a long time ago. She still clung to her faith in science. But her grip was loosening bit by bit, shock by shock.

All she could say now was, "We'll see, Mulder. We'll see." She changed the subject. "Think Humphreys wants to join us?"

"He wants to play around with the equipment," Moore said. "See if he can patch it up." He turned toward the trees. "Let's go."

Scully and Mulder followed Moore into the forest. It was slow going. Then they hit an open space. Suddenly the late afternoon sky spread wide above them.

Tree stumps filled the clearing. The stumps were fresh. A few tall pines still lay where they had been felled.

"The men were hard at work—right to the end," Moore commented.

"Busy as bees," agreed Mulder. Then he paused. He was staring up at a towering pine on the edge of the clearing. "Speaking of bees, are there many in this neck of the woods?"

"Not many," Moore said. "Why?"

Mulder pointed to a branch of the pine.

Something that looked like a big gunnysack was hanging from it. But its dirty gray strands weren't made of cloth.

"Could be a hive," said Moore, scratching his head. "Or maybe some kind of cocoon."

"A hive?" said Mulder. "A cocoon? What kind?"

Moore shook his head. "I can't say for sure. I've never seen anything exactly like it."

"I think I can make out something inside it," Scully said. "See that dark shape?"

"Hard to tell from here," said Moore, squinting.

"We'll have to investigate," Mulder said. "How about it, Scully? Want to give it a spin? You're the scientist."

For Scully, there was only one way to respond to a challenge. "Love to," she said. "Let's figure out how I do it."

"Shouldn't be hard," said Moore. He took a long rope out of his pack. "We can rig up a harness for you. Throw the rope over that branch. And haul you up there. Then you cut that thing down. Mulder's right. You're the best one to do it. You're the lightest. The branch can support your weight."

"As usual, women and children first," said Scully. "Well, I've been wanting to test out this hunting knife." She patted the brand-new knife in its brand-new sheath on her brand-new belt.

The rope harness that Moore rigged up was

crude but effective. It went around Scully's waist and under her armpits. Moore got the loose end of the rope over the branch on the third heave. He and Mulder pulled at it and Scully rose into the air.

This is fun, Scully thought. Then her smile faded. The sack was coming closer and closer. And the closer it came, the nastier it looked. Its grimy gray strands glistened with some kind of grease or slime. It certainly seemed to be a cocoon. But Scully didn't like to imagine what kind of creature had made it.

"Can you reach it?" Mulder called from below.

"Just a little bit more!" she called.

Another pull, and it was in range of her knife blade. She reached out her arm as far as she could. She started to saw away at where the cocoon was joined to the branch.

Then her knife hand froze.

Her stomach did a slow somersault.

Something was sticking out of the gap she had carved.

A bony human finger.

"You see something?" shouted Mulder.

"Yeah, I do!" she managed to shout back.

"What is it?" Mulder asked.

"Let me take a better look," she forced herself to answer.

Scully felt the rope yank.

She moved closer to the opening.

She squinted past the finger into the cocoon.

Staring back at her were two empty eye sockets. She was face-to-face with a skull.

"So what do you see?" Mulder shouted.

"You take a look!" Scully shouted back. She finished cutting the cocoon loose. It fell to the ground by the two men's feet.

Mulder and Moore wasted no time in hauling Scully down. Then they turned toward the cocoon. By the time Scully was free of her harness, Moore had cut the cocoon wide open.

"Oh my God," said Scully, looking down.

Inside the cocoon, was a body. It was the size of a baby, curled up inside its mother. But it was definitely not a baby. It was shriveled and shrunken, almost mummified. Or like an orange that had been sucked dry.

But what had it been when it was alive? And how long ago had that been?

"Time to go to work, Scully," Mulder said. "This one looks right up your alley."

Scully gritted her teeth. She reminded herself that she was a trained scientist. She had a medical degree as well. This was just another job. She reached down and touched it.

"It's hard and dry," she announced. She wished she felt as calm and cool as her voice. "Almost as if it's been preserved."

"Or embalmed," suggested Moore.

"More like all the fluids were bled from the body," Scully observed. "Like it's been—cured." She gave the corpse another close look. "It's a male, I think."

Meanwhile Moore was examining the cocoon. "I'd say it's some kind of spider's nest," he said. "Some kind of insect cocoon, anyway."

"And what kind of insect could have gotten a man all the way up that tree?" Scully wanted to know.

All three looked up at the branch high above.

All three shook their heads.

Chapter SIX

Back in the deserted camp, Humphreys was whistling while he worked. He was finishing his repair job on the broken electric generator. It gave him a good feeling to do his best for the Schiff-Immergut Lumber Company.

Schiff-Immergut had been good to Humphreys. It had given him his first job after high school. It had promoted him year after year. It had paid for his station wagon, his ranch house, his two kids' college tuition. It covered his medical bills and would take care of his retirement when he got old. He owed everything to the lumber company. In return, he gave it his all.

He was screwing in a new spark plug when he heard a noise outside. It wasn't loud, but Humphreys wasn't a top security man for nothing. He had ears like a cat's.

He moved fast as a cat as well. He grabbed his shotgun. Then he was out of the generator shed to see who the intruder was.

Humphreys didn't know whether it was a man or a grizzly invading the camp. It didn't matter. He stroked his shotgun. Both chambers were loaded.

He was just in time to see the cabin door closing behind someone or something. He pumped his shotgun. He leveled it and kicked the door open.

The tall, rangy man stood by the table, with his back to the door. He paid no attention to the sound of Humphreys' kick. He was too busy grabbing moldy food with his bare hands and wolfing it down.

"Freeze!" shouted Humphreys. "Turn around slowly—with your hands in the air."

The man stuffed one more handful of food into his mouth. Then, without hurrying, he obeyed.

His bearded face was framed by long, matted, dirty brown hair.

"Doug Spinney," Humphreys snarled. "I ought to shoot you where you stand."

Spinney, unfazed, looked wearily at Humphreys and his gun.

"Might as well shoot yourself, too, Humphreys, old pal," he said. His voice was as empty of fear as his eyes.

"You're in no position to be testing me," Humphreys warned him. "Now talk fast, Spinney. What the devil happened to my men?"

"What men?" Spinney asked.

"The men working in this camp," said Humphreys, fighting to keep his trigger finger still.

Spinney shrugged. "I don't know what happened

to them. Not for sure. But I can make a good guess."

"And what's that?" demanded Humphreys. He raised his shotgun so it was pointed right between Spinney's eyes.

Spinney looked into the barrels without blinking. "The same thing that'll happen to us when the sun goes down," he said.

Suddenly a voice demanded, "What's going on here?"

It was Mulder. He stood at the open cabin door. Behind him were Scully and Moore.

Reluctantly Humphreys lowered his gun. "This animal is Doug Spinney," he said. "The man who did all this monkeywrenching. And a murderer. I'd like to make him pay right now."

Scully just had to take one look at Spinney to recognize him. He was one of the monkeywrenchers in Mulder's slide show. She wondered where Spinney's sidekick Teague was hiding.

"I'm no murderer," Spinney protested.

"You're a liar," snarled Humphreys, raising his gun.

Mulder put his hand on the barrel and gently pushed it down.

"We're investigators—not executioners," he told Humphreys. "Let's hear what Mr. Spinney has to say."

"We stand here taking much longer and there

won't be anything left to say," Spinney said. "We've got to get that generator started. The darkness is our enemy."

"What are you talking about?" Humphreys barked. "Stop the horse manure."

Spinney ignored him.

"Any of you want to give me a hand?" he asked. Without waiting for an answer, he calmly shoved Humphreys' gun aside and walked out the door.

Openmouthed, Humphreys watched him go. It took him a moment to get back his balance. His hands tightened on his gun. He started for the door.

Mulder raised his palm to stop him. "Not so fast, Humphreys," he said. "I have a hunch he knows what he's doing."

"Him run the generator?" sneered Humphreys. "He just knows how to smash things, not make them work. I'm the one who had to pick up the pieces and try to put them back together."

"But he seems to be the only one who can put the pieces of this puzzle together," said Mulder. "I say we help him."

He went out the door after Spinney.

"Agent Mulder has a funny habit of being right about things like this," Scully said, and followed him.

Humphreys exchanged looks with Moore.

"We'd better go along," he told the forest service

agent. "We don't want to leave Spinney alone with those two. He's too good at selling his line of phony goods. Especially to folks from the beltway who don't know any better."

When the four of them caught up with Spinney, he was holding a five-gallon gas can.

"Putting sugar in it?" asked Humphreys. "Or have you decided to burn the camp down?"

"Piece of advice, Humphreys. Keep your mouth shut—and your eyes and ears open," said Spinney.

He hauled the gas over to the generator. The others followed, watching his every move.

"What did you mean about the darkness being our enemy?" Mulder asked him.

Spinney started pouring the gas into the generator fuel tank. "That's when they come," he said, not looking up.

"When *who* comes?" asked Mulder.

Spinney finished pouring, set the can down, and screwed the fuel tank cap back on. "They come from the sky," he said. "Can take a man right off his feet. Devour him alive. I saw it happen."

"Happen to whom?" Mulder asked.

Spinney ignored the question. "God, I hope this works," he said, gripping the starter rope of the generator. He gave the rope a sharp, powerful yank.

Scully, watching him, found she was desperately hoping the generator would start, too.

She didn't know why, but she sensed she would soon. She would find out why light in this forest suddenly seemed the most precious thing on earth.

Chapter SEVEN

The generator turned over once. Twice. And roared to life.

Scully ran her fingers over her forehead. She realized she had been sweating.

"I need to eat," Spinney announced. "I haven't eaten in three days."

Without another word, he headed for the cabin.

Humphreys turned to the others. "What a line of bull that guy puts out. As if any of us would believe a word of it," he said.

The other three were silent.

"Hey, what's with you?" Humphreys asked. "I tell you, Spinney wouldn't tell the truth if his life depended on it."

"We found something in the forest," Scully told him.

"What?" said Humphreys.

"A man caught in some kind of insect cocoon," Moore said.

"A cocoon?" said Humphreys.

"Or something," Mulder said.

"I never saw anything like it," Moore admitted.

"We have to find out exactly what it was," said Scully.

"We have to get some more answers from Mr. Spinney," Mulder declared.

Scully looked at the cabin. The windows were glowing in the dusk.

"Well, at least we know the lights are working," she said.

"And we know he turned them on the second he got into the cabin," Mulder said. "He was more eager to get light than food."

The four of them went into the cabin. They found Spinney opening up cans of franks and beans. He had already finished off the moldy food on the plates.

Spinney looked up and gave the security man a crooked grin. "Got a beef, Humphreys?" he asked. "Worried about me eating company property? Believe me, that's the least of Schiff-Immergut's worries in this neck of the woods. Not to mention ours."

"Speak for yourself, Spinney," Humphreys said. "You're the one who's going to have worries."

"You mean, when we get back to civilization?" Spinney said. "I don't see that as a pressing problem right now." He went back to spooning cold beans into his mouth.

Mulder sat down across from him. "I have some

questions for you, Mr. Spinney," he said.

"I'll make some tea," Scully offered. "It's going to be a long night."

"Yeah," said Spinney between mouthfuls. "Nights are long around here. Real long."

Moore sat down at the table, too. Humphreys kept his shotgun on his knees, and his eyes on Spinney's every move.

"What happened to you out here?" Mulder asked.

Spinney took his time answering. He finished his can of beans and opened another. He wiped his mouth with the back of his hand and belched loudly. Then he said, "We're camped two valleys over. Four of us. Three now—after last night."

Humphreys spat. The blob of spittle hit the plank floor near Spinney's feet. "No wonder things smell funny around here," Humpheys said. "These woods are filled with skunks."

"Filled with worse things than skunks, believe me," Spinney told him. Then he turned back to Mulder. "Our Jeep has a dead battery. We drew straws to see who'd hike over here and swipe one that works from the loggers."

Humphreys started to say something. But Mulder silenced him with a sharp look.

"Why didn't all of you just hike out of the forest?" Mulder asked Spinney.

"It's more than a day's hike," Spinney said. "No way we wanted to be out in the forest at night. Not after what happened to Teague."

"Teague is the man who was—devoured alive?" asked Scully, as she poured them all tea.

Spinney nodded, remembering. He pushed his can of beans away. He had lost his appetite.

"So what are you guys doing up here?" Mulder continued.

Spinney raised his eyebrows in phony innocence. "Camping," he said.

"Yeah, sure," Humphreys said. "The kind of camping you do is a federal offense."

"Hold off for a second," Mulder told him.

But Moore took Humphreys' side. "He's right," he told Mulder. "This man is a criminal. He could be placed under arrest."

"He could be—and should be," said Humphreys.

Spinney and his pals were on too many wanted posters for him to waste his breath defending his innocence. Instead he went on the attack.

"And what about you, Humphreys?" he demanded. "What about the crime against nature you commit?"

"We operate completely under the law," Humphreys said. "We pay for the right to take those trees and after we do, we—"

Spinney cut him off. "I got news for you, Mr. Law and Order. Your loggers were taking trees nobody has a right to. Trees here for hundreds, even thousands of years. Trees that are marked. Trees that are supposed to be protected. Except that out here nobody is looking. Or maybe they're looking the other way. So don't talk to me about breaking the law, *sir*."

Moore leaned forward. "Schiff-Immergut loggers were taking marked trees?"

"You bet they were," Spinney assured him. "Marked in bright orange by your own people. The big no-no for cutting. Or am I wrong about that, Mr. Forest Service Man? Are you maybe more interested in greenbacks than green space?"

Moore's face flushed. He turned to Humphreys. "Old growth trees. You know anything about that, Steve?"

"No. Of course not," Humphreys declared.

But Moore kept looking at him. Looking at him hard.

"You're going to take *his* word over *mine*?" Humpheys said indignantly.

Moore said nothing. But his silence said a lot.

Humphreys got to his feet. "I'm not going to sit here and take this bull," he snarled. Angrily he stomped toward the door.

Spinney leaned back in his chair and watched

him. A strange smile was on his face.

"You don't want to go out into the night, Humphreys," he warned ever so mildly. "Take my word. It's out there."

Humphreys paused with his hand on the doorknob. He chuckled.

"What?" he said. "If I walk out this door I'm going to be attacked? By something that will eat me alive? And then spin me in its web?"

Spinney's smile grew broader. "Yes," he said.

Humphreys chuckled harder. He had to pause for breath before he said, "And this *thing*, I suppose it's too polite to come inside to get me."

"For some reason it's afraid of the light," Spinney told him quietly.

"It's *afraid* of the light?" Humphreys was gasping with laughter now.

Moore interrupted his fun. "There might be something to what he's saying, Steve."

Humphreys stopped laughing. His voice was grim. "You know what I think? I think this man is a liar and a murderer. I think he's just clever enough to make up a story like this. Even to whip up that phony cocoon thing. Just to monkeywrench anybody who wants to take any trees. And I'm going to prove I'm right."

He swung open the door.

He stepped out into the night.

He was holding his shotgun at the ready.

Spinney leaned back in his chair. "You can't say I didn't warn him," he said.

Mulder went to the open doorway to look out into the night. Scully followed, and the others came after her.

Scully heard a series of strange buzzes. Sharp little sounds, quick as the blink of an eye.

"What's that?" she wondered aloud.

"An insect zapper," Mulder said. He pointed at a brightly lit device hanging outside the cabin. "It attracts bugs at night. Then it fries them. A swarm must have hit it at once."

"Lots of bugs in the woods," Scully said.

"Lots and lots of bugs," Spinney agreed. "They're part of nature's great plan. When we kill them, we upset the balance. Just like with almost everything we do out here."

The sound stopped as suddenly as it had begun.

The night was filled with silence.

Then they heard Humphreys' mocking voice.

"Come out, come out, wherever you are!"

Chapter EIGHT

The next morning, Humphreys was still crowing. The whole group was sitting at the breakfast table. They were finishing flapjacks and coffee that Moore had made.

"Hey, Spinney," Humphreys taunted, "The boogeyman didn't get me, did he? And the cookie monster didn't eat me up. I didn't even run into the big bad wolf. I wonder why."

"You know, Humphreys," Spinney said with disgust, "I saw macho men like you in Vietnam. They'd go out on night patrol in the jungle. They'd come back laughing. 'A piece of cake,' they said. Then one night, they wouldn't come back. We'd have to go out to find them. And ship them home in body bags."

"You were in Nam?" Moore asked. The forest service agent looked surprised. "I didn't figure that."

"Yeah, I was there," Spinney said. "Jerk that I was. I was one of the guys who dumped poison on the jungle. You remember, Agent Orange. Then I saw what it did to the trees. And to the people. I swore I'd make up for it. I'd stop the destruction of Mother Earth. Even if I had to fight another kind of war to do it."

"I was in Vietnam, too," Moore said. "And I'm proud of it. I was there to do my duty. Serve my country. Protect its way of life. Preserve its laws. Just like I'm doing now."

"You serve your country," said Spinney. "And I'll serve mine."

"There's just one country," Moore said.

"So you say," Spinney sneered.

"So I know," Moore replied.

Scully listened to the two men argue. The Vietnam war had ended a long time ago, when she had been a little girl. But for these two, it was still going on. She had a hunch it was never going to end for them.

Mulder spoke her thoughts when he said, "Let's forget Vietnam. We're in a different war now. Against a different enemy. And we're all in it together. I suggest we head out into the forest. See if we can pick up traces of the missing men. Figure out what happened to them. We don't want to waste any daylight."

"And I say we don't waste any more time," Humphreys said. "There's nothing out there but a bunch of trees. Trees that this sicko values more than human life. I'm going to see him tried on murder charges."

Humphreys turned to Moore. "Come on, Larry. What say we march this monkeywrencher back to civilization. Put him behind bars where he belongs."

Moore gave Humphreys a level look. "I need more evidence. And a few answers, too. I want to take a closer look at those trees that were cut down."

"Do you really?" Spinney said. "I'll show you one of them. I warn you, though. You'd better have a strong stomach."

"I tell you, you can't trust a word this guy says," protested Humphreys. "He lies like he breathes."

"I'm not asking you to believe my words," Spinney said. "Just your eyes."

"It's like following a crooked Pied Piper," grumbled Humphreys. But he joined the others following Spinney out of the cabin.

Spinney knew exactly where he was taking them. He did not hesitate as he led the way through the forest.

"Here we are," he announced. "Take a look at this. A good look."

"My God," Scully said, wide-eyed. "What a tree!"

"You mean, what a hunk of dead wood," Spinney corrected her.

The tree lay on the forest floor. It was at least a hundred and fifty feet long. Its trunk was more than ten feet in diameter.

"This redwood was standing here since time

began," Spinney said. "Until a bunch of greedhead men came and cut it down."

While Spinney stood smiling bitterly, Scully and Mulder walked along the tree's length. They had never seen a giant like it before.

Moore squatted by its base. He carefully inspected the bright orange *X* spray-painted on its side.

"Who marks these trees?" Scully asked him.

"Federal Forest Service," Moore answered. "You're only allowed to cut trees marked with a blue *X*."

"You must get a lot of lumber from a big tree like this," Scully remarked.

"Thousands of board feet," Spinney said. "It's a lot easier than taking smaller, young trees. A lot cheaper, too. They make tons more money with these giants."

"Stop, or I'll start crying," said Humphreys sarcastically. He turned to Scully. "Let me remind you, these monkeywrenchers often mark trees with their own paint."

Moore looked up from the orange *X*. His eyes were hard. So was his voice. "This tree's five hundred years old if it's a day, Steve."

Mulder was more interested in the tree stump. "Hey, take a look at this," he said.

The excitement in his voice drew them all to the

stump. Their eyes followed Mulder's finger. It went across the rings in the wood from the outside inward. Then it stopped. It rested on a ring that was thicker than the others. And a different color as well. Not brown, but sulphur yellow.

"What would this ring be?" Mulder asked Moore.

"I don't know. I've never seen one like it before," the forest service agent said.

"These center rings. These are the oldest ones, right?" Scully asked.

"Yeah," Moore said. "Every ring represents a season of growth. You can count them to see how old the tree is. And measure them to get an idea of the temperature and rainfall. But I don't know about this yellow one. I should take a sample."

"Are we finished with our nature walk?" asked Humphreys. "Because I just want to know one thing. What happened to my loggers?"

"That's what we're trying to find out," said Scully.

"By looking at a tree stump?" Humphreys demanded. "It's this monkeywrencher you should be looking at. Look inside him—and you'll see he's guilty as sin. He's the one who offed my people."

"I don't think he did it," Mulder said calmly.

"Well, I think he did," Humphreys said. His hands tightened on his shotgun. His voice was loaded with menace. "I want him arrested. And I mean right now."

"There's no rush," Mulder said. "He's not going anywhere."

"Not with a gun on him," said Humphreys, pointing his weapon at Spinney. "But what if his two buddies show up while you're poking around? Remember your forest service buddies who vanished?" he asked Moore. You can imagine what the monkeywrenchers did to them."

"I have to take a core sample of this tree, Steve," Moore answered.

"I got families down there who want answers about their loved ones," Humphreys insisted. "So do you, Larry. Answers you're not going to find in that tree. We've got a crime to solve, and the faster the better."

"The death of that tree's the only crime to investigate," Spinney said.

Humphreys looked at Moore. Then at Mulder. Then at Scully.

He made one last try at winning them over. "Come on, you guys. Don't let this killer pull the wool over your eyes."

No one said a word. Or made a move.

"If you wimps feel like that," Humphreys said angrily. He turned and started striding away.

"Where are you going, Steve?" asked Moore.

"I'm going to hike back down to your truck," Humphreys said over his shoulder. "And get on the horn. Get some people up here. People who'll take action."

"Steve!" Moore called after him.

But he had already vanished in the trees.

"Let him go," Spinney said. "Let him find out for himself." He smiled. "And he will. Just as soon as the sun goes down."

Chapter NINE

The sounds of Humphreys stomping through the forest faded. He was gone.

Moore returned to the tree stump.

"Let's see what we can find out—before sunset," he said. "I'll bore out a sample from the core. We can take a good look at it back at camp."

"Sounds good to me," Mulder said. "The yellow ring might give us some answers."

"I hope so," Scully said. "All we've found so far is questions."

Spinney shook his head. "You people won't listen to me, will you? You won't believe what I've seen. As for myself, I just have one question. Do we have enough gas for the generator? Can we get through the night?"

When they got back to camp, Spinney said, "I'm going to the generator shed. Check out the fuel supply."

The others followed Moore into the cabin. He set his tree sample, a cylinder of wood the size of a long pencil, down on the table. Then he squinted at it through a magnifying glass. "This is odd," he said.

"Something odd in this case?" said Scully. "Surely you jest."

"What is it?" asked Mulder.

"This yellow ring," Moore said. "It's got something living in it. Some kind of tiny bug. It doesn't make sense."

"Why not?" asked Scully. "Lots of insects live in trees."

"Right," said Mulder. "What makes this bug so strange?"

"Insects attack a tree in different ways," Moore explained. "But they always invade the living parts. The leaves. The roots. The new growth rings."

"Maybe they're borers of some kind," Mulder suggested.

"They still wouldn't be working so deep in the tree," Moore said. "Here, take a look for yourself." He handed Mulder the magnifying glass.

Mulder looked through it. He saw what Moore was talking about. Crawling over the yellow wood were countless mites. Mites too small for the naked eye to see. Mites unlike any Mulder had ever seen. They looked like miniature spiders.

"Maybe the wood in this ring is different," Mulder said. "They seem to be feeding on it. Take a look, Scully. You might know what they are."

He passed her the magnifying glass.

She peered through it and shook her head.

"Never saw these in any textbook," she said. "Can you identify them?" she asked Moore.

"They seem to be wood mites of some sort," Moore said. "But nothing I've run into before. I can't really explain them."

I can't really explain them. The sentence made Mulder's eyes gleam. Scully knew why. Mulder was on home turf now. His favorite hunting ground. X-files territory.

"Could they have been living in that tree for hundreds of years?" he asked. "Maybe even longer?"

"I don't see how," Moore said. "The yellow ring was too close to the core. A tree provides water for its outer rings only. Insects need water to survive."

"Insects that we know about," Mulder said.

Meanwhile, Scully was taking another look through the magnifying glass.

"It appears they might be hatching out of the wood," she said. "Maybe when you took this sample, you disturbed their nest."

"Can they build a cocoon?" a voice cackled from the doorway. It was Spinney.

"Now listen up, lawpeople," he told them. "I've been in this forest awhile. I know these trees like I know my friends. And I know what's going on here."

"And what do you say is going on?" Moore asked.

"I'll tell you—if you're willing to listen to a monkeywrencher," Spinney said.

"Come on, Spinney," Moore said. "It's too late in the day to start playing games."

"You're right about that—it is too late in the day," said Spinney. He had stopped joking. Nightfall was something he didn't joke about. "My pal Teague died just after that tree was cut down," he told them. "Right about then the loggers disappeared, too."

"You think these mites are what killed them?" Scully asked.

"Maybe they've been lying asleep for hundreds of years," Spinney said. "Maybe thousands. Maybe they woke up hungry."

Spinney paused. No one said anything. They were all busy thinking about what he had said.

Spinney grinned. "You know, I almost miss old Humphreys. It feels funny not hearing him laugh like a donkey. I wonder if he's still laughing now."

Many miles away, Steve Humphreys wasn't laughing. He was cursing.

It was still daylight when he reached the road. But daylight was fading fast.

The truck was where they had left it. He glanced at the two blown tires. Driving on the tire rims would ruin them. But it would get him out of the forest.

He swung open the driver's door. He tossed his

shotgun onto the front seat. He climbed behind the wheel and reached out to turn the ignition key.

His fingers closed on empty air.

"Rats," he muttered. "Where is it?"

He looked on the sun visor. Nothing. In the glove compartment. No luck there either.

He looked out the window. The last of the daylight was going.

"Here's something at least," he said to himself. He pulled a flashlight from the glove compartment.

He turned it on just as darkness descended.

He shone it out the window. The night was huge. The flashlight beam looked pitiful.

But it would do. It would give him enough light to see what he was doing. He'd hot-wire the engine. Then he'd be out of this cursed place.

He went to work under the dashboard. Good thing he knew how to take care of Number One, he thought. Maybe he wasn't any Vietnam hero. Though it wasn't his fault he wasn't drafted. Not with his wife expecting a baby. But he'd like to see any of those vets beat his survival skills. He was a guy who knew the way the world worked. It was the law of the jungle. Dog eat dog. Only the fittest survived. The weak ones got eaten.

He got hold of the ignition wires. Here we go, easy as pie. He smiled, and touched the wires together. His smile grew as they sparked. He heard the engine turn over. Once, twice—

Then it died.

Rats, he thought. Must be damp or something. He tried again. Again the wires sparked. Again the engine turned over. Once, twice, three times—

Then silence again.

He climbed out of the truck. He opened the engine hood. He played the flashlight beam over the engine. He'd find what was wrong. Fix it. And—

Hmmmmmmmmmm.

The humming came from the forest. It rose, then fell away.

He straightened up. He turned his flashlight toward the sound.

He saw nothing. Just trees. Endless trees.

He grabbed his shotgun from the cab of the truck. Pointed it at the trees.

The humming rose again. But from a different direction.

He whirled around, shotgun in one hand, flashlight in the other.

"You monkeywrenchers come out now," he shouted. "You ain't scaring me. I know what you're up to."

The only answer was more humming. Louder and louder.

Then Humphreys' mouth dropped open. The

flashlight dropped from his hands.

He didn't bother picking it up. He had all the light he needed. The forest edge was flooded with light. Green light. Dazzling. Hovering above the treetops.

As he watched openmouthed, the cloud broke up into glowing pinpricks. And they came swarming down toward him.

Humphreys blasted away with both barrels of his shotgun.

The humming drowned out the echoes of his shots.

He threw away his gun and dashed into the truck, slamming the door. He rolled the windows shut. Then he tried the ignition wires again.

The engine turned over once, twice—and roared to life.

"Go, baby, go," he urged between clenched teeth. The truck started to move, staggering like a drunk on its flat tires.

Looking out the window, Humphreys saw the points of light close up. They were bouncing against the glass.

Some kind of bug, he thought. Bugs that glowed green in the dark.

But he'd soon be rid of them. He'd soon be out of this—

Aghhhh!

He screamed as he felt the first bite on his hand.

Only then did he see the bugs streaming in through the air vent.

Even as he watched, the whole cab filled with them. They covered him. Every inch of exposed skin. His hands. His face. His neck. He flailed away but they ignored him. Their bites burned and stung like hot needles.

"Gotta get out of here!" his mind screamed. He turned the door handle. It was jammed.

There was no way out.

No way.

No—

"Noooooo!"

His last living sound merged with the humming that ruled the dark.

Chapter TEN

In the cabin, the lights stayed on.

Scully kept studying the tree sample. She was a scientist who never gave up on a problem.

Mulder went to make himself more tea. He believed in relaxing his mind, and letting answers come to him.

Moore stood looking out the window. He was anxious for Humphreys to get back. Whatever their differences, Humpreys and he had been friends for years.

Spinney was the only one in the cabin smiling. He enjoyed seeing Moore's worry grow.

"Humphreys should have been back by now," Moore said. "I know Steve. He gets hot under the collar. But then he cools down. He wouldn't cut out on us. He's a team player."

"Why don't you go out and look for him?" Spinney asked.

Moore didn't answer.

"On the other hand," Spinney said, "why bother? What could happen to a good old boy like your good old pal? A tough guy like him who isn't afraid of the dark?"

From the table, Scully announced, "These bugs aren't moving anymore. They're either dead or asleep."

"Don't count on them being dead," Spinney told her. "Or asleep. It's the light. They don't like the light."

"That's weird," Scully said. "Bugs are usually attracted to the light."

"These are not your usual bugs," Spinney said. "Or haven't you noticed?"

Meanwhile, Mulder noticed something else unusual.

He ran his finger over a kind of grease that covered the wood countertop in the cooking area.

He had seen the same layer of grease on the refrigerator.

He checked out the rest of the kitchen space. The grease was everywhere. Either the loggers had been the sloppiest cooks in the world, or—?

Or what?

He didn't know. He filed the question in the back of his mind. It was like putting aside a piece of a jigsaw puzzle. It might not fit in now. But it would later, when a few more pieces fell into place.

"Scully," he said, "You know much about insects?"

"Got straight *A*'s in biology," she said. "But that was a while ago."

"What do you remember about them?" Mulder asked.

"Let's see," Scully said. "They're a key link of the chain of life. You could even call them the foundation of all life on earth. And there are a lot of them."

"They outnumber humans, right?" Mulder asked.

"To put it mildly," Scully said. "Something like two hundred million bugs for every human on the planet."

"And they've been around a long time," said Mulder.

"Much longer than us," Scully told him. "Even long before the dinosaurs. Six hundred million years is the latest guess. Why?"

Mulder moved to the table. He looked at the sample from the tree. He touched it gently, with respect.

"This tree's how old?" he said. "Five, six, seven hundred years?"

"Yeah. That old at least," said Moore.

"And these rings show changes of climate?" Mulder said.

"Right," said Moore.

"That means something strange happened in the year that this yellow ring was formed," Mulder said.

"Looks like it," agreed Moore.

"What kind of strange thing?" wondered Scully.

"I'll make a guess," said Mulder. "A volcanic eruption. Volcanoes still hit this mountain chain. All the way from Washington to Oregon. Remember Mount Saint Helens? The whole mountain just blew its lid one day."

"How would that explain the bugs?" asked Scully.

"Look at Mount Saint Helens," Mulder said. "When it erupted, radiation was released. It came from deep inside the earth. Suddenly strange things started to grow."

"What kind of strange things?"

"One was an amoeba they found in a lake," Mulder said. "No one had ever seen anything like it. It could suck a man's brains out."

"Don't bother telling me how they found it," Scully said. "I can imagine." Then she shook her head. "A brain-sucking amoeba. That's too weird. I know you, Mulder. Sometimes your stories are just too much."

But Mulder got back-up.

"It's true," said Spinney. "In Spirit Lake. There are documented accounts of what happened to swimmers. You're right, Scully. You don't want to hear the nasty details."

"Okay, I'll buy that," Scully said. "But an amoeba is a one-celled life-form. It can mutate fast. Bugs are different. They're complex living things.

Thousands of cells. A mutation would take years, decades, even centuries. Try again, Mulder."

Mulder's eyes went remote. Scully could almost hear his brain working, whirring like a computer.

"Then maybe what we have here isn't a mutation," he said finally. "What if they're some kind of insect eggs? Thousands, maybe millions of years old? Eggs from deep inside the earth. Eggs that volcanic eruptions brought to the surface? Eggs sucked up into the tree through its root system? Eggs lying quietly in the tree for hundreds and hundreds of years—"

"Until those loggers cut down the tree—and those eggs hatched." Spinney finished Mulder's line of thought. "Yeah, hey, good thinking, Mr. F.B.I. Man."

Spinney turned to Moore. "That would be a good joke, wouldn't it?" he said to the forest service agent. "Or maybe joke isn't the right word. Maybe justice is. Yeah. Poetic justice. Those loggers break the law. And let loose the things that kill them."

Spinney paused. "And maybe take out your friend Humphreys."

Moore didn't answer.

"And maybe us," Spinney finished. "Maybe us, too."

Chapter ELEVEN

Doug Spinney woke up at dawn the next day. He woke with a start. He had been having a nightmare. A nightmare of bugs tearing at his old buddy Teague's flesh. Teague's screams filling the forest. While Spinney and his other pals watched and could do nothing.

Spinney's eyes were still glazed with horror when they opened. Then they blinked and focused. He saw the first pale light of day through the dirty cabin window. He had made it through another night.

He looked up at the ceiling. The light in the cabin was still on. The generator had made it through the night as well.

He looked around the room. The others were still asleep. They hadn't had nightmares to wake them. Not yet.

He climbed to his feet quietly, careful not to wake them. He stole out of the cabin, closing the door softly behind him.

As soon as he was outside, he started moving fast. He half trotted across the camp to the generator shed. The generator was still going. He didn't bother to shut it down. He didn't want the lights going off in the cabin. It might disturb the others inside. They'd turn off the lights fast when they awoke. They had enough sense to do that at least. That way, the generator would have enough gas to last another night.

Spinney picked up the five-gallon can of gas and shook it. He felt its weight and heard the gas inside sloshing around. There wasn't much left. But it would do. It had to.

He carried the can out of the shed to one of the monkeywrenched trucks. He raised the truck hood. From the utility belt around his tattered Levi's he took a crescent wrench. Quietly and carefully he loosened a bracket. It was the bracket that held the truck battery in place.

He put the wrench back in his belt. Eagerly he reached for the battery.

There was a sharp click behind the back of his head. Spinney froze. He knew what it was. A pistol being cocked.

He turned and looked into the barrel of a pistol. A .45 calibre F.B.I. issue.

"Going somewhere?" Mulder asked, his gun pointed between Spinney's eyes.

"Hey, man, you're quiet," said Spinney. "You would have done good in Vietnam. 'Course, I'm not as sharp as I once was. Used to have eyes in the back of my head."

"I'm sure your war stories are quite interesting," Mulder said. "But they're not what I'd like to hear now. I'll ask my question again. Going somewhere?"

"Me? Why you ask that?" Spinney said. His eyes were darting, looking for a way out. He couldn't see one. All he could see was Mulder's pistol pointed dead at him. And Mulder's gaze, just as pitiless.

"Seems a funny time to do an auto repair job," Mulder said. "Tell me if I'm wrong—but were you planning to cut out of here?"

Spinney thought of lying. He didn't think about it long. Mulder wasn't the kind of guy you wanted to lie to. He might seem nice and gentle on the outside, but below the surface of this F.B.I. agent, Spinney sensed something else. Something as hard and unyielding as a rock. Spinney didn't know what it was. But he didn't want to test it to find out.

"Okay, okay," Spinney said. "I'll level with you. I gotta go save my friends. They're still trapped in the middle of the forest. They only have enough gas to keep their generator going four hours tonight. Six hours max. They're dead if I don't get back there with this gas."

"And what about us?" Mulder asked. "Our generator. You didn't seem worried about it."

"It's got enough to run as long as you need it,"

Spinney said. " I checked. It'll keep going until I can get you all out of here."

"Get us all out?" said Mulder. "That's real good of you. One detail, though. Mind telling me how you're planning to do it?"

"With this truck battery," Spinney said. "It still works, see. The only one in camp that does. We blew up all the others, but by the time I hit this truck, it was getting late. The sun was almost down."

"Shame on you," Mulder said. "They should strip you of your monkeywrench."

"Hey, look, let bygones be bygones," Spinney said. "I want to square things now."

"How?" asked Mulder, still keeping his pistol level.

"Me and my pals, we've got a Jeep," Spinney said. "It's parked just two valleys over. All it needs is a battery. I could get to it. And be back here tomorrow morning. We could all drive out, easy as pie."

"Sounds good," said Mulder.

"Sounds good because it is good," Spinney affirmed.

"One little question," Mulder said. "If it's the way you say it is, why the sneaking around? Why didn't you just tell us your plan?"

"It's Moore. The Freddie—the forest service guy," said Spinney, shaking his head.

"What about him?" said Mulder.

"He wouldn't go for it," Spinney said. "He'd never trust me. I'm not one of his lumber company friends. Far as he's concerned, I'm an outlaw. Doesn't matter if it's the lumber company breaking the law. I'm the one who isn't making people money."

"You think he's taking bribes," said Mulder. "You have evidence?"

"Nahh," Spinney said. "I don't. And he's probably not. It's just the way straight arrows like him think. If you got a corporate logo, you're one of the good guys. If you make waves, you're bad."

"And me?" said Mulder. "Why do you think I'd believe you? Remember, I'm F.B.I."

"You may be a G-man," said Spinney, "but you're not like any I've ever seen. You don't have tunnel vision like most of them. You're weird, man. Weird enough to see things the way they are in this weird world. You should come over to our side. Or maybe you already are."

"Not exactly," Mulder said. He had to keep back a smile. But that didn't stop him from keeping his gun steady.

"Look, man, trust me," Spinney pleaded. "Maybe I've done some stuff you don't agree with. Maybe

I've bent a few rules. Maybe I've even broken the law once or twice or three times. But there's a reason behind it. It's about the preservation of life. I ain't never killed anybody. Not since Vietnam, anyway. That place cured me for good. And now I'm asking for a chance to save you and your friends. You gotta let me. You gotta believe me."

"And if I don't?" Mulder said.

"You know what'll happen," said Spinney. "You've seen it. Come on, what do you have to lose?"

"With you going off with the last of our gas?" said Mulder. "That cuts our odds of surviving. They go from bad to worse. They go to zero."

"It's a gamble you have to take," Spinney urged.

Mulder bit his lower lip.

Gambling with his own life was one thing.

Gambling with the lives of others was something else.

Spinney gave him a big yellow-toothed grin.

"Hey, man, scout's honor I come back," he said. "What do you say?"

Chapter TWELVE

Mulder didn't like to think what would happen if he was wrong about Spinney. Or if Spinney was wrong about being able to get back to them in his Jeep.

But he couldn't stop thinking of it.

He couldn't stop remembering the human remains in the cocoon.

He couldn't stop wondering how many other cocoons there were.

He couldn't stop counting off the number of people who had vanished here: the loggers a few weeks ago, the forest service men sent to look for them, the loggers fifty years ago, before there were laws protecting ancient trees. How many more cocoons were there? How many more victims, down through the years, as men felled the giant trees, woke the wrath of nature, and brought it down on their heads?

Mulder couldn't just sit and wait for Spinney to get back. He had to do something. Try to, anyway.

He found a tool kit in one of the trucks and took it into the cabin. The others were starting to stir. He ignored them. He went straight to the smashed radio, and started to take it apart.

"Didn't know you were a techie, Mulder," said Scully, getting up and rubbing her eyes.

"I used to fool around with ham radios when I was a kid," Mulder said, not looking up from his work.

"Let me guess why," said Scully. "Ever succeed in making contact with a spaceship?"

It was a private joke between them. Only Scully knew Mulder's story of how his younger sister had been kidnapped when he was a child. Kidnapped by alien beings. How he had seen it happen. How no one would believe him. How it had set him on the trail of all kinds of strange sightings and stranger disappearances. A trail that had finally led him to the X-files.

"No," said Mulder. "But it wasn't from lack of trying."

"I can bet," said Scully, as she watched Mulder at work. Mulder wasn't one to give up on anything. No matter what the odds, or how long it took.

"Want some tea for breakfast?" she asked.

"Sure, thanks," he said, not pausing. By now the radio was in pieces. He started putting it together again.

"Make some for me, too, please," said Moore.

The forest service agent got to his feet and stretched. He went to the sink and splashed cold water on his face. Scully gave him a mug of tea, and he took a sip.

"Thanks," he said. "What's your partner doing?"

"Tinkering with the radio," Scully said.

"Wasting his time," Moore announced. "He'll be at it all day."

"Tell him that," Scully said.

Moore shrugged. "He might as well do that as nothing. Myself, I'll check out the camp. I want to make sure old Spinney isn't up to mischief. One thing's for sure, though. He's not running away. Not him. Funny thing. A guy who says he loves trees—scared to death of the forest."

Moore had just left the cabin when Mulder announced, "Radio's back up."

He touched two wires together. With a buzz of static, the radio came back to life.

Scully hurried to the table. "It's working?"

"Sort of," said Mulder. "It's not getting any reception. The receiver was beyond repair."

"But is there transmission?" she asked. "Can you send out a message?"

"I'll give it a whirl," said Mulder. He picked up the microphone, then flipped a switch on the radio a couple of times until the static held steady. He moved the dial to an emergency frequency. Then he spoke loudly and clearly into the mike. "This is a call for help. Is there anyone on this frequency?"

There was only more static.

"As I said, no reception, I can only keep broadcasting and hope someone picks us up."

Scully smiled wryly. "You know that riddle?" she said. "If a tree falls in the forest with no one to hear, does it make a sound? I guess we're going to find out the answer."

Mulder spoke into the mike. "This is Special Agent Mulder of the F.B.I. with Special Agent Scully. We have an emergency. We have a suspected outbreak of life-threatening insect infestation. We have a possible quarantine situation. Our position is—"

Mulder paused. Scully thrust a map of the region in front of him.

But before he could read off their bearings, the static died. The radio face went dark.

"The generator's quit," was Scully's guess.

"Come on. Let's check it out." Mulder put down the mike and stood up. He clicked off the safety on his gun as he and Scully left the cabin.

They arrived at the generator to find Moore there.

"What happened to the generator?" Mulder demanded.

"I turned it off," Moore said.

"Well, turn it back on," Mulder said impatiently.

"I've got the radio working."

"What happened to the gas can?" asked Moore.

Mulder hesitated. He swallowed. Then he said, "*Spinney* took it."

"Spinney took it?" said Moore in a stunned voice. He shook his head as if someone had slapped him in the face.

"Early this morning," said Mulder. "He took a truck battery, too."

"He's gone?" said Moore, still trying to digest the news. "When did you find him and the stuff he stole missing?"

Mulder hesitated a moment before he admitted, "I let Spinney go. He's going to come back for us tomorrow morning."

"Really," said Moore. "Did he give you his personal guarantee of that?"

"He gave me his word," Mulder said.

"His *word*," Moore snapped. "And what do you think his word is worth? The word of a man who has made an art of sabotage? The word of a man who defies authority? The word of a man who laughs at the law? The word of a man who probably put a bullet through my windshield?"

"It was a judgment call," Mulder said.

"I question that judgment," Moore said. "I call it crazy."

"What would you have done?" asked Mulder.

"I would have stopped him in his tracks," Moore said. "Dead or alive."

"At least this way there's a chance we can get out of here alive," Mulder argued. "That's one more chance than we had before."

"Or one less," Moore said.

"What do you mean?" Scully wanted to know. She wished she could back Mulder up. But when he went this far out on a limb, it was hard to do.

"Your good-hearted partner let Spinney leave with the last of the gas," said Moore. "This generator's got about a quarter of a tank left. Maybe less. We'll be lucky if we make it through the night."

"What about the gas in the trucks?" asked Scully.

"Since Spinney isn't here to tell you, maybe Mulder here will," Moore said with disgust.

"Mulder, what's the score?" asked Scully.

"There is no gas," Mulder told her. "The tanks have all been ruptured. Or filled with sugar."

"By the same man we're supposed to trust to come back and save us," said Moore.

"Then we've got to keep trying on the radio," Scully decided. "We've got to get a Mayday message out. There has to be someone on the emergency frequency. Someone to hear us."

“Want to bet your life on it?” said Moore. “Every drop of fuel we use to run the radio is fuel we'll need tonight. I don't want to be praying somebody got our message when the tank hits empty at two A.M. And the generator quits. And the lights go out. Do you?”

“So what do we do?” Scully said.

“Ask your partner,” Moore said. “He's the one with all the brilliant answers.”

Their eyes turned to Mulder.

“Whatever we can,” he said. “Before darkness falls.”

Chapter THIRTEEN

"We have to circle the wagons," Mulder declared. "We have to turn the cabin into a fortress."

"Against what?" asked Scully.

"Against the night," Mulder said. "Against whatever's out there in the night."

"Wish we knew exactly what it was," Moore said. "It's like fighting blindfolded."

"Nobody ever said it would be easy," said Mulder. "Come on. Let's find out what we have to work with. We can rummage through the camp. One thing you have to say about Western civilization. It produces a lot of useful junk. Maybe we can recycle some of it."

It was Scully who spotted what they needed. A pile of dirty plastic sheets in the camp garbage dump. Logging equipment must have come wrapped in it.

"Beautiful," said Mulder. "We can make ourselves snug as a bug in a rug. Except that 'bug' isn't the word to use."

They carried the tarps into the cabin. There they found hammers and nails. They got to work nailing the tarps over the floor, the walls, the ceiling.

"Be sure not to leave any cracks exposed," Mulder cautioned them.

"Looks like we're doing our friends' work for them," Scully said, as she nailed down a tarp over the window. "We're building a cocoon of our own. With us in the middle of it."

"That's the problem with building defenses," Mulder agreed. "You want to protect yourself. But you can wind up trapping yourself."

"One more thing to check out," Scully said. The lone lightbulb in the cabin hung down from the ceiling on a long cord. It was in easy arm's reach. She started to unscrew it.

"Be careful," said Moore. "It's the only bulb we've got. The lumber company seems to have cut corners in this camp."

Scully nodded. She held the lightbulb as if it were a very thin-shelled egg.

"You know that new kind of bulb? The kind that only needs changing every seven years?" she asked.

"Yeah," said Moore.

"Well, this isn't one of them," Scully said. "It isn't even a name brand. I think the filament is starting to go. I hope I'm wrong."

"We'll find out soon enough," said Mulder, as Scully screwed the bulb back in. "The sun's going down."

"I'll go start up the generator," Moore said.

"Better move fast," said Mulder. "You don't want to be outside when it gets dark."

"Agreed," said Moore, already halfway out the door.

He was back in three minutes flat. He must have run all the way. Breathing hard, he nailed the last tarp over the door.

"Truth time," said Mulder. He snapped on the light switch.

No one breathed until the light came on.

Mulder looked at his watch. "Sunrise is about ten hours away."

"With the tarp and the light together, we should make it," Moore said.

"No problem," Mulder agreed. "Unless—"

"Unless?" said Scully.

"There are some surprises," said Mulder.

He lay down on a bunk. Moore lay down on another, and Scully on a third.

"Funny, I used to think I hated TV," Scully said. "I wouldn't mind the tube now."

"It would sure beat staring at that bulb," agreed Moore.

"And listening to the generator," said Mulder. They could hear the generator humming in the distance. "My imagination, or is its sound going up and down?"

"I did the best I could to fix it," said Moore. "But

it's still not working smoothly. We can just pray it doesn't conk out."

"We don't have to hear it to know how it's working," said Scully. "We just have to look at the lightbulb. It keeps flickering. Watching it makes me feel like I'm on a roller coaster."

"Try getting some shut-eye," Mulder suggested.

"Easier said than done." Scully felt her stomach tighten as the bulb dimmed. It brightened and her stomach unknotted.

She decided to take Mulder's advice. She shut her eyes. But she opened them quickly. Darkness wasn't what she wanted to see.

She turned over onto her stomach. She looked away from the bulb. She fixed her gaze on a tarp covering a wall. Suddenly she sat up, almost banging her head on the bunk above.

She tried to keep the panic out of her voice. "I can see them—through the tarp. Come look."

She led the way to the tarp. Dots of green light glowed through the dirty plastic. Hundreds of dots.

"They're coming through the walls," Scully said. "Down near the floor. Where the light doesn't reach. I want to get a better look at them."

She pressed both hands against the tarp and started smoothing away the wrinkles.

"Aaaaah!" she screamed.

The glowing green dots were on her arm, crawling up it.

"They're on me!" she shrieked. "Get them off!"

She leaped back, arms flailing.

"Watch it!" shouted Moore, as one of her hands hit the lightbulb.

It flung through the air, swinging out of control.

Moore almost knocked Scully down as he dashed for it. He caught it gently, then brought it to a safe stop.

Meanwhile Mulder had his arms around Scully. He could feel her shaking wildly. She was as out of control as the lightbulb had been.

"Scully," he said. "It's okay. It's okay."

"Get them off!" she pleaded.

"Stop it!" Mulder commanded. "Calm down. Stand still."

Scully forced herself to obey. She stood with her fists clenched, her arms stiff at her sides. Her heart was beating like a hammer. Her eyes were shut. She couldn't bring herself to open them.

"Where are they, Mulder?" she asked. "Do you see them?"

"They're not just on you, Scully," Mulder said. "They're everywhere. They've been leaving the slimy grease that's all over the cabin. I think they lit up on your arms because you were in shadow."

"I thought we were safe here," said Scully. She shook her arms to make sure they were free of bugs. They were. Or seemed to be. At least nothing was biting.

"There's a good chance we're okay," Mulder said. "Just a few of them don't seem to do damage. And it looks as if light keeps them from swarming."

He glanced at the window. "I don't want to think how many of them it would take to devour a human being. How many of them might be out there. Filling the sky. Covering the trees. Getting hungrier and hungrier."

"Let's just hope they make these things well in Taiwan." said Moore, still holding on to the lightbulb. Dawn is still a long way away."

Chapter FOURTEEN

Scully did not even try to go to sleep. She was trembling too hard. There was only one way she knew to calm down.

She had to get back to work. She lay on her bunk and thought about the case.

Suddenly a thought struck her.

She got up and went to her backpack. She took a glass jar from it and set it on the table.

"I thought so," she said to herself.

She turned and said to the others. "Come here. Take a look at this."

Mulder and Moore joined her. They looked at the glowing dots of green light inside the jar. There were about a dozen. They flew furiously fast, as if struggling to escape.

"I collected these in the forest, from the cocoon we found," Scully said. "They appear to be like fireflies. If that's the case, the light they give off comes from waste from their bodies. When the waste hits the air, it produces a glow. In this case, a green glow."

"Right," Moore said, nodding. "A chemical reaction from instant oxidation."

"Except these aren't fireflies," said Mulder,

squinting into the jar. "Fireflies don't look like tiny spiders. Fireflies don't make cocoons. Fireflies don't suck the life out of you."

"That must be how they make their cocoons," Scully said. "After they feed, they have to get rid of waste. It mixes with their own juices. They squirt it out. It hits the air with a glow. And it turns to strands of greasy gray fiber."

"Judging from the cocoon we found, they're hungry little devils," said Moore. "They must suck every last bit of nourishment from their prey."

"You'd be hungry, too," Mulder said, "if you hadn't eaten for centuries."

"They're making up for lost time now," said Moore.

"I wonder how many there are," said Scully.

"No telling," said Mulder. "But I'd guess in the millions. There had to be that many to take care of thirty loggers. Trouble is, that may not be the worst news."

"What is?" said Scully.

"I have an idea they're multiplying by the minute," said Mulder. "The more they eat, the faster they breed. When they found those thirty loggers, they hit the jackpot. It was a feast for them, and it must have set off a population explosion. Insects are like that. That's why they outnumber us by so much."

"But they've never eaten humans before," said Scully.

"There's always a first time," said Mulder.

"And this one could mean the end of human life," Scully said grimly. "Other species have disappeared in the past: the dinosaurs, the mastodons. We're still not sure why. But we do know there were volcanic eruptions that disturbed the earth. They could have set off a plague like this one. It could be our turn now to be the victims."

"We also know meteors from outer space have hit the earth," Mulder said. "They could have brought deadly life-forms with them."

"Whatever their origin," said Scully. "these insects are a threat to human life."

"They're a threat to our lives for sure," said Moore.

At that moment, the electric light flickered. In the distance, the hum of the generator faltered.

"Oh God," said Scully, her fists clenching. Cold sweat beaded her skin. In her mind was a picture of the bugs swarming, closing in on them. Feasting on them.

Then the light steadied. So did the hum of the generator.

Scully wiped the sweat off her forehead.

"Maybe we'll make it through the night," said Mulder.

"Maybe," said Moore.

"But then what?" Scully wondered. "It's over a day's hike out of the forest. We could never make it before nightfall. By now the bugs must be ranging all over the woods, looking for food. If they find us outside after dark, we're dead."

"Maybe somebody heard our radio call," said Mulder. "Help could be on the way."

"You sent that call hours ago," Scully said. "Help would be here by now."

"Stands to reason," agreed Moore. "The forest service has choppers. So does the lumber company."

"Well, I'm not giving up on Spinney," Mulder insisted. "He gave me his word he'd come back to get us."

"Spinney talks a good game," said Moore. "What he does is something else. I've been playing hide-and-seek with him for years. I've read all the pretty words in all the pamphlets he puts out. I've seen all the ugly damage he causes. I'm not buying anything he says. And I'm sure not staking my life on it."

"Moore is right," said Scully. "Spinney isn't exactly a Boy Scout. We can't count on him. We have to figure out what to do if he doesn't show."

"And we can't wait around too long hoping he will," said Moore. "Every minute of daylight will be precious."

"Any ideas?" Scully asked Mulder.

"Don't worry," he said. "We'll think of something."

"When?" asked Scully.

"When the time comes," said Mulder.

Moore looked at his watch. "The time is coming closer every second."

"And those bugs are getting hungrier," said Scully.

"Still hours until dawn," said Mulder. He yawned. "I don't know about you, but I'm getting some shut-eye."

"Good idea," said Moore. "We'll have to be clear-headed when dawn comes. Tough choices to make."

"If we're still alive when dawn comes," said Scully.

"Well, pleasant dreams," said Mulder, going to his bunk.

"I could use some," said Moore, sacking out, too.

Scully lay down on her bunk as well. But she didn't shut her eyes. Mulder might act like Mr. Cool. As for her, she was chilled with fear. She didn't feel like she would ever sleep again.

She stared up at the electric light. She told herself that as long as it stayed on, she was safe. It was like a life raft in a sea as dark as night.

She let her mind drift. She tried not to think of the bugs, the cocoon, the hideous shrunken corpse.

Then everything went dark.

She opened her mouth to scream.

Then she realized her eyes were closed. She had fallen asleep.

She opened her eyes and saw the bulb was still working. But it was dim.

Brighter light edged the dirty plastic covering the windows.

Dawn had come.

Chapter FIFTEEN

An hour later, the day was not much brighter.

Morning mist filled the forest. It would take another hour or more for the sun to burn through.

Moore wasn't waiting. He looked at his watch and said, "That's it. Spinney's not showing. We're on our own."

He turned to Mulder. "You got us into this, Mr. F.B.I. Got any bright ideas about how we get out?"

"I've been thinking," Mulder said.

"Don't tell me," Moore said sarcastically.

"I want to check that truck," Mulder calmly went on. "The one that Spinney lifted the battery from."

"Why bother?" said Moore. "It's a wreck. Sugar in the fuel line. Battery gone. Tires slashed."

"Let's just take a look," Mulder repeated.

He headed for the truck, with Moore and Scully following. He circled around it, kneeling at each wheel in turn. He was examining the tires.

"This is the best of them," he said, pointing at the front right one. "It's practically new. The tread's barely worn. And the slash isn't bad. The tube is just nicked."

"Yeah," said Moore. "The monkeywrencher must

have been lazy. Or else arm-weary by the time he got to it."

"Is there a patch kit back in your truck?" Mulder said.

"Yeah," Moore said. "It's still there. Untouched. There was no use trying it. The tires were beyond repair. The caltrops totaled them."

"But we could use it to patch *this* tire," said Mulder. "Then we could replace one of your ruined tires with this one, and the other with your spare. It might not last long. But maybe long enough for the truck to limp out of the forest. Get us in the clear before nightfall."

"Hey, it might work," said Scully.

"And if it doesn't," Mulder said with a grim smile, "at least we can use the truck radio. Warn the people outside what's up here. Save them from what happened to us."

"Right," Scully agreed somberly. "Stop them from being the bugs' next meal."

"It beats waiting here," said Moore. "No way the generator will last another night."

"Let's get rolling," said Mulder. "Rolling the tire, I mean. We can cut straight through the forest. It's a lot more direct than following the winding road to the truck."

"We'd better hurry," said Moore. "We have no time to waste."

Mulder went to the driver's cabin. He came out with a tire iron and a jack.

In minutes the tire was off the truck. Mulder rolled it in front of him as he jogged into the mist.

"Brrrr," said Scully as they jogged. "It looks like ghostland."

Around them the trees loomed like dark giants. The fog swirled around the trail ahead. But as they ran, it began to lift.

By the time Moore took his turn rolling the tire, the sun had broken through. By then they had slowed from a run to a quickstep.

"Wish we didn't have to go so fast," Scully remarked. "This forest is beautiful. It makes you feel good to be alive. Be nice to walk through it. Well, maybe some other time." She paused. "When our little insect friends are gone. If they're ever gone."

She glanced admiringly at the huge old trees. Through the deep green of the pine needles the sky was a brilliant blue.

"It's God's country," Moore agreed. "I've loved it since I was a kid. I can't think of anything better than making sure my kids can grow up loving it, too. For me the forest service was the only way to go. I could never see working for just a paycheck. You have to work for something more than money."

"Funny hearing that from you," said Scully. "You

sound like you're on Spinney's side. You know, saving the trees and all. Yet Humphreys is your pal. Not Spinney."

Then she said, "Hey, my turn with the tire."

Moore passed it to her without breaking stride.

"Humphreys and I are on the same side of the law," he said after a moment. "Spinney wants to take the law into his own hands. That's not the way we do things in this country."

"Let's try jogging again for a while," Scully suggested. "The path is wide here. We can run three abreast."

"I'm with you," said Moore. "Still lots of ground to cover. We'll be cutting it close."

"It's looking good, though," said Mulder, glancing at his watch. "We should get to the truck by late afternoon. Then, if there are no hitches—" He paused, then said, "Well, we'll cross that bridge when we come to it."

As they started to jog again, Scully asked Moore, "But you still think Spinney is the only one who plays fast and loose with the law? Seems to me that Humphreys is no angel either."

"I don't like to think that," Moore said. "I've known Steve for years. We golf together, play tennis together, our families have barbecues together. I always figured I could trust him like a brother."

"That's the problem with enforcing the law,"

Mulder said, jogging alongside Moore. "You can't afford to get too friendly. Not with anybody you may have to collar."

"Sad but true," agreed Scully. "Our jobs set us apart. With no one to trust but the people we work with. It can get kind of lonely. You have to believe in what you're doing."

"You have to really believe," agreed Mulder.

"Like Mulder does," said Scully. "Right, partner?"

They exchanged quick grins. It was a private joke.

Moore's face stayed grim. He wiped away sweat from his eyes. The day was getting hot as the sun moved across the sky. Its dazzling glare exploded like flashbulbs through the treetops.

"I suppose friendship could have clouded my judgment," he admitted. "Maybe I didn't notice as much as I should have. Maybe I didn't look as hard as I should have. When I see him again, I'll make sure he levels with me, pal or no pal."

Scully stopped in her tracks.

"Tired?" asked Moore.

"We can take a break," said Mulder.

"It's not that," said Scully. "A thought just hit me. Humphreys headed for the truck when he cut out. What if he managed to drive it out of here on its rims? What if there's nothing waiting for us? Nothing but the bugs?"

"The possibility already crossed my mind," Mulder confessed, "but I decided there was no sense worrying about it. Staying in the camp, our odds of survival were zip. This way, at least we have a chance."

Scully didn't bother asking what kind of chance. Mulder had made it crystal clear. It was better than nothing. Barely.

"Come on," she said, rolling the tire again. "Last one to the truck is a rotten egg."

They continued moving through the forest in silence. Silently they shifted from jogging to quick-step when the trail narrowed again. Silently they passed the wheel from one to another. They had run out of talk. They were all too busy thinking the same thing.

It was late afternoon when they reached the highway.

Scully gave voice to the relief they all felt.

"Thank God," she said. "There's the truck. It's still here."

Chapter SIXTEEN

Funny how fast things turned around, thought Scully. As fast as a rug pulled out from under your feet. One second, she was overjoyed to see the truck. The next, the truth hit her. It felt like a punch to the jaw.

"The truck," she said. "It's plowed into a tree."

Moore had already seen it. He led their dash toward it. He reached it steps ahead of the others. He looked into the driver's cabin.

He turned around and said to Scully, "Better not look, lady."

"Don't worry. I'm used to—" she started to say.

That was as far as she got before she took a look.

Her mouth dropped open.

She saw Humphreys' face pressed against the inside of the glass. Part of his face, anyway. Part of a face twisted in horrible pain.

The rest of his face, his head, his whole body, was wrapped in a dirty gray cocoon. The cocoon filled the driver's cabin.

Scully turned away. She did not want the others to see her face turn a pale shade of green. She took pride in being an agent who always kept her cool.

She need not have worried. Moore and Mulder looked pale and queasy themselves.

Mulder recovered first.

"Humphreys made a good try—but no cigar," he said.

"Poor devil," said Moore. "He was a good guy at heart. Maybe just a little too loyal to his company. Whatever he did, he didn't deserve a punishment like this."

"Nobody does," said Mulder. "But when you mess with nature, justice turns blind. And everybody gets punished."

"Right. Everybody," echoed Scully. Her stomach had stopped turning over. But she still did not feel very good. Especially when she looked westward.

"The sun sure sets early around here," she remarked.

Off in the distance, the sun hovered, glowing above the rim of the mountains.

"I guess that's it for us," she said.

Moore nodded. "Nowhere to run."

"And nowhere to hide," Mulder said.

Scully brightened. "Maybe we can take refuge in the truck," she said.

But before anyone could answer, she shook her head. "Dumb idea. The truck is full of bugs. They'll swarm to life looking for dinner as soon as it's dark."

"I've got a flashlight," said Moore. "Maybe we can use it against them."

This time Mulder shook his head.

"You don't want to try it," he said. "There'd be too much shadow for them to swarm in. And you'd be trapped in a small space when they do. You'd wind up like Humphreys, with your face squashed against the glass. Better to take your chances with nothing caging you in."

"Doesn't really matter," said Scully. "The end result will be the same. It'll take a miracle to save us."

Nobody argued.

They stood there in silence, staring at the setting sun.

Then they all heard a distant sound.

A miraculous sound.

It came from up the highway, from the direction of the mountains.

The sound grew more distinct.

"It's a car," said Moore. "But who—?"

"I think I know who," Mulder said, grinning. "And I think it's a Jeep."

Minutes later, they saw the Jeep, coming toward them. Spinney was at the wheel.

He was driving full-out. He braked to a screeching, skidding stop when he reached them.

He didn't waste words.

"We've got to get moving," he said. "I wasted enough time, looking for you in that camp. Hop in."

"But look, we've got a body," Moore protested. "Humphreys' body." He motioned toward the truck. "We can't leave him here. He's got a wife and kids. They'll want to give him a decent burial."

"We're the ones who'll need burying if we don't move," Spinney said, his voice harsh with impatience.

Then he saw the pain in Moore's eyes. Humphreys and Moore had been friends. He looked at the truck. It was easy to imagine what had happened to Humphreys. Spinney had seen the same thing happen to his friend.

"Don't worry about Humphreys," Spinney said, his voice turning gentle. "I had a radio back in my camp. I sent out a call for help. There'll be people coming in. They'll take Humphreys. I just hope for his family's sake that the coffin stays closed."

Moore nodded. He gave one last look at the truck, and went to get his gear. He and the others tossed their stuff into the Jeep. Then Moore climbed in beside Spinney, and Scully and Mulder got in the back.

They had barely closed the doors when Spinney roared off. He pressed the accelerator to the floor.

The Jeep tore over the rough road, bouncing like a bronco. Mulder shouted a question to Spinney over the noise of the engine. "Your friends? You found them?"

Spinney kept his eyes on the road, his foot to the floor. "Yeah, I found them!" he shouted back. "They didn't make it! But we will, by God!"

Scully looked at the forest whizzing by. It already lay in darkness. The long shadows of the trees edged the road. The lower rim of a bloodred sun dipped below mountains black as ink.

She saw that Spinney had turned on the headlights, and she opened her mouth to shout a question to him. Would they make it?

She closed her mouth without a word. There was no sense asking. They would find out soon enough.

Suddenly there was a loud sound. An explosion even louder than the motor.

A jolt ran through the Jeep.

It started bouncing crazily.

"No, no, it can't be," moaned Spinney.

Desperately he struggled with the steering wheel, fighting to keep the Jeep from careening off the road.

It steadied, then slowed, as he braked it to a stop.

He got out, taking a flashlight with him. By now he needed it. There was a faint reddish glow in the west. But everywhere else night had fallen.

Spinney shone his flashlight on the right front

tire. Slowly he shook his head.

Mulder turned to Scully in the backseat.

"Five'll get you ten that the tire is ripped to shreds," he said.

"Same odds on what did it," Scully said.

"The monkeywrencher's best friend," said Mulder. "A caltrop."

They could read Spinney's lips muttering, "Clean forgot about it."

"Talk about shooting yourself in the foot," said Moore.

Then he said, "This I have to see. If it's the last thing I ever do, I want to make sure Spinney eats crow."

He opened the Jeep door and stepped out into the night.

"No!" Mulder shouted at the top of his lungs. "Get back inside! Close the door!"

Moore froze, bewildered.

"Get back in!" Mulder shouted again.

"Please!" Scully shouted in chorus.

"Wha—?" Moore started to ask. Then his mouth gaped open like a fish.

He heard Spinney screaming. He turned and saw what Mulder and Scully had seen.

Spinney was bathed in blinding green light.

The bugs had scented their food.

They had swarmed.

And arrived.

Moore stayed frozen in shock.

Mulder moved fast.

He flung open the door. He leaped out of the Jeep. He shoved Moore back into the front seat and slammed the door on that side. He tore around the rear of the Jeep and slammed the driver's door. Then he jumped back inside beside Scully, slamming the door behind him.

"But Spinney—" Scully said.

"Too late," Mulder said, panting, as they all looked out the window.

Spinney's flashlight lay on the ground, still glowing. Spinney's arms flailed uselessly. He ran blindly away from the Jeep, taking the glowing green swarm with him.

Down the highway, beyond the headlights, Scully could see the green light. It hovered motionless a few minutes. Then she saw it growing larger, coming closer.

"The bugs finished off their appetizer," said Mulder. "Now they're coming back for the main course."

Chapter SEVENTEEN

The light almost blinded Mulder.

He blinked, trying to focus, trying to think.

His first thought was: The light, it's not green.

His next thought: it's daylight.

Then he saw the eyes looking down at him. They were shielded by clear plastic. The man bending over him wore a hooded white cleansuit. He looked ready to go on a moon walk. Every inch of him was covered, protected from all contamination.

Gloved hands lifted Mulder out of the Jeep. He saw other men in cleansuits standing by. A short distance away were the three large white vans that had brought them here.

"Thank God you're alive," the man said. "When I got that stuff off your face, I held my breath until your eyes opened. What the devil happened?"

"It's a long story," said Mulder.

"We got a few pieces of it on a radio call," said the man. "From some guy named Spinney. Said something about bugs. Deadly bugs. Is he around here? Maybe he can fill in the details."

"I'm afraid not," said Mulder. He remembered his last sight of Spinney, running screaming into the dark. "You might find what's left of him up the road."

Mulder shut his eyes. He tried to piece together what had happened.

He saw again the three of them in the Jeep. Moore in the front seat. He and Scully in the back.

For a few minutes they'd thought they were safe.

Then glowing green bugs had come pouring through the air vents in the dashboard.

They'd reached Moore first. Helplessly Scully and Mulder had watched them feasting.

Then some of them had broken off from the others. They'd swarmed toward the back. Mulder remembered the first stabs of pain when they reached his skin. He remembered Scully's shrieks of agony in his ear.

Then why was he still alive? Mulder wondered. Why hadn't they sucked the last drops of life out of him?

He couldn't remember. He had blacked out as the wave of pain crested.

Could the insects in the Jeep have been spread too thin with three victims to attack?

Had the edge been taken off their appetites after Spinney and Moore and—

Mulder's eyes flew open.

"There's someone else in the backseat. My partner,

Scully," he croaked. He was too weak to move. He could barely turn his head. He could only ask, "Tell me, is she alive?"

"I didn't see her," the man said. "But I may have missed her. I barely spotted you. And then I was in a hurry to get you out. The whole inside of the Jeep is draped in some kind of strange fiber. Almost like a cocoon. Not to mention the slimy grease over everything."

Mulder heard a voice shout, "I've found two more. I'm looking for life signs."

A second voice said, "I think I see some movement in this one. Around the face. Maybe a mouth breathing. Or trying to speak."

The first voice said, "Let's get this stuff off of it."

A moment later, the second voice said, "It's a female."

"Alive?" the man with Mulder shouted to them.

"Affirmative," said the second voice. "But I don't know for how long."

Then Mulder heard another voice. It must have been talking into a radio.

"We have an emergency evacuation situation," it said. "Urgently requesting a helicopter. Also prepare a quarantine facility. We have at least two victims of an unidentified infection. Or else exposure to unknown biological agents. They are to be handled with extreme care. Also a total news blackout.

Definite potential for a deadly epidemic. And extreme danger of a public panic."

Let's see how good medical science really is, was Mulder's last thought before he passed out again.

"Who are you?" Mulder asked the man in the white cleansuit bending over his bed.

"Dr. Simmons, from the Center for Infectious Diseases in Atlanta," the man said. "I was flown in to take over your case three days ago."

"And where am I?" Mulder asked.

"Hyman Rickover Naval Hospital, Seattle, Washington," Simmons said. Then he added, "You can keep talking. You seem to be strong enough. But keep on breathing though that oxygen tube in your nose."

Mulder took a long drag of oxygen, then looked around him. "This is a special ward, I take it," he said.

"A very special ward," Simmons said. "You're a very special case."

Mulder's bed was in a large white plastic dome. Attendants in cleansuits stood guard at the entrance. Others monitored high-tech medical equipment. Mulder turned his head and saw two other beds beside his. It figured. The medicos had three very special cases on their hands.

"How are you feeling?" Simmons asked.

"I think I'll live," Mulder said. "But you probably know better than I. Any test results yet?"

"Your respiratory charts are good," Simmons said. "That was our big worry. We thought that you might have breathed in a harmful material. But what we found wasn't that dangerous."

"What did you find?" asked Mulder.

"A sizable amount of a chemical called luciferin," Simmons said.

"Which is what?" Mulder wanted to know.

"The same enzyme found in fireflies and similiar insects," Simmons said. "Our experts are still trying to determine exactly what species you encountered. So far, no success."

"And what about the others?" Mulder asked. "Moore. And Scully."

"Moore's life is hanging by a thread. A very thin thread," Simmons said. "Medical science can do only so much when dealing with the unknown."

"And Scully?" Mulder said.

"As I said, it's difficult to give you a definite—" Simmons began.

"Can I take a look at her?" Mulder requested.

The doctor hesitated. Then he said, "I don't see why not. Just keep breathing in that oxygen."

Mulder carefully got out of bed, the tube still in his nose. It was hooked up to an oxygen tank in a cart. He wheeled it with him as he followed Simmons to Scully's bed.

He looked down at her.

She lay still as death. Only a faint rise and fall of her chest showed she was breathing. Her face was blotched red with countless bites. Her features were gaunt, wasted away.

"Scully?" Mulder said softly.

"She's still not out of the woods—if you'll pardon the expression," said the doctor. "She's lost a lot of fluids. If there had been a few more insects, or if they'd had a few more hours, no way could she have made it. As it is—" Simmons paused, then went on, "We're doing the best we can. But there are no guarantees in a case like this."

"And I told her it'd be a nice trip to the forest," said Mulder.

The pain he felt now wasn't from insect bites. But it was just as piercing. It was a bad case of serious guilt.

"No way you could have known," the doctor assured him. "No way anyone could have known. A totally bizarre phenomenon."

"Yeah, a natural for the X-files," said Mulder, half to himself, and half to the body in the bed.

Then he asked the doctor, "How are you going to seal off the forest? What if the swarm migrates?"

"The government is giving it the highest priority," Simmons said. "They're using every available means of insect control—their whole arsenal of pesticides, plus carefully controlled tree burning. They're quite certain they'll be successful."

Mulder couldn't keep from smiling a crooked smile. Spinney must be turning over in his grave.

And he couldn't resist asking the doctor, "What if the government's best efforts fail?"

"Don't even think about it, Agent Mulder. They won't fail," the doctor said crisply. "It's out of the question. Completely unthinkable."

The doctor turned sharply and strode away.

Mulder sighed.

The people in charge were always the same.

They did not like questions that had troubling answers.

They did not want to think the unthinkable.

Mulder looked down at his partner.

"Please get better," he said. "I'm going to need all the help I can get."

He might have been crazy, but he thought he saw her head give a tiny nod.

He'd have to wait and see.